MEET THE CREW

WRITTEN BY MELINDA LA ROSE ILLUSTRATED BY ALAN BATSON

DISNEY PRESS
New York

MEET JAKE

"Yo-Ho, Let's Go!"

MEET IZZY

"PIXIE DUST, AWAY!"

MEET CUBBY

"AW, COCONUTS!"

MEET SKULLY

"CRACKERS!"

MEET CAPTAIN HOOK

"SAVE ME, SMEE!"

MEET SMEE

"AYE, AYE, CAP'N!"

Ahoy, mateys! Do you want to join my pirate crew? Then just say the pirate password, "yo-ho-ho!" As part of my crew, you'll need to learn the Never Land pirate pledge.

TODAY'S PIRATE PLEDGE

Never borrow something without asking permission. And be sure to return what you borrowed.

JAKE AND THE SPYGLASS

Captain Hook and Smee are searching for treasure on Pirate Island.

"**BLAST IT**, Smee! There's nothing but seashells on this seashore," says Captain Hook. "Where is all the treasure?"

"Oh, these pretty shells are a treasure of their own," says Smee. "Don't you think so, Cap'n?"

Just then, Captain Hook notices something shiny in the water.

"Look alive, Smee," says Hook. "There's treasure out there on the water! Give me my spyglass."

"Oh, dear," says Smee. "I'm afraid I . . . I don't have your spyglass, Cap'n."

"You lost my spyglass?" asks Captain Hook.

"It would seem so, sir," says Smee. "But don't worry, Cap'n. We can row out in the dinghy and see what that shiny thing is for ourselves."

"I have a better idea," says Hook. "We can row out in the dinghy and see what that shiny thing is for ourselves."

"It's this way," they each say, pointing in opposite directions.

"Without that spyglass," says Hook, "we can't see where we left the dinghy."

On another part of the beach, Izzy, Cubby, and Skully are collecting seashells.

"Wow, the tide sure brought in a lot of shells," says Izzy.

"They're so pretty," says Cubby.

"I wonder what else might wash in with the tide?" Jake says. "I'm gonna take a look with my trusty spyglass."

Why did the lobster steal the spyglass?

"WHEW," says Cubby. "It's getting hot."

"Yeah, really hot!" agrees Izzy. "I know! Why don't we go swimming and cool off?"

"Great idea, Iz," says Jake.

"YAY-HEY, LET'S PLAY," says Izzy.

"Last one in is a rusty anchor!" says Jake.

"Wait for me!" calls Cubby.

Because he was being shellfish!

"Why is it so hot on this infernal beach?" asks Hook.

"We could always take a little swim, Cap'n," suggests Smee.

"I don't want a little swim," says Hook. "I want to find the dinghy and go get that treasure!"

Just then, Captain Hook hears something.

SPLISH, SPLASH!

"Do you see what I see, Smee?" asks Hook.

"Oh, yes, Cap'n," says Smee. "Those sea pups are having such fun splashing around! Please, can we go for a dip?"

"No," says Hook. "It's Jake's spyglass on that towel.

Quick! Hide before they see us!"

"But, Cap'n," says Smee, "if we ask the sea pups nicely, maybe we can borrow their spyglass to find our dinghy."

"Why borrow the spyglass when we can take it?" says Hook. He uses his fishing hook to try and nab the spyglass.

"Can you see without your spyglass, Cap'n?" asks Smee.

"I see perfectly fine," answers Hook.

YOINK! OOPS! Hook nabs a life preserver instead.

"Good thinking, sir," says Smee. "That'll come in handy when we find the dinghy."

Hook tries again. **YOINK!** This time he grabs a seashell. "Not a spyglass, sir," says Smee. "But it *is* beautiful."

"OUCH!" yells Hook as a hermit crab comes out of the shell and pinches his nose.

"**BLAST AND BARNACLES!** We're going to have to do this the old-fashioned way," says Hook. "Run!"

Hook runs onto the beach and grabs the spyglass.

"**CRACKERS!**" says Skully. "That not-so-sneaky snook just ran off with our spyglass!"

"Which way did he go?" asks Cubby.

"I don't know," says Jake. "Without our spyglass, we can't see that far!"

"Leave it to me," says Skully. He flies up high in the air and spots Hook and Smee getting into their dinghy.

"DINGHY, AHOY!" calls Skully. "Thataway!"

"Hurry, mateys, into the rowboat," says Jake. "We'll catch them in the water!"

"HEAVE-HO!" calls Jake.

"It's no use," says Cubby. "We can't paddle in this strong wind!"

"I've got an idea," says Izzy. "Give me those towels!"

Izzy ties the towels together to make a sail!

"We'll ride the wind right over to those pirates!" says Izzy.

"It's working," says Cubby.

"Awesome," says Jake. "We'll catch that dinghy in no time!"

"Smee, you slowpoke, can't we go any faster?" asks Captain Hook.

"Sorry—ugh—Cap'n," says Smee. "This wind is blowin' mighty hard. Maybe we'd go faster if you helped me row?"

"Help you row?" says Hook. "You just need to work harder. Put your back into it! We're almost at the shiny thing!"

"Aye—ugh—aye, Cap'n," says Smee.

Why did Hook paint his picture on the crow's nest?

"Well, hello, Captain," says Jake. "I think you have something that belongs to us!"

"We'll be taking that spyglass back now," says Skully.

"I hope you find what you're looking for," says Cubby.

Hook is surprised. But then he remembers the shiny thing. "Who needs their spyglass when there is treasure upon us!"

He wanted the crew to look up to him!

"Look, Cap'n, it's your spyglass!" says Smee.

"At least *something* has gone my way today!" says Hook.

Hook looks through the spyglass and sees . . . a giant eye!

"Smee, what is that?" asks Hook.

"Uh, Cap'n, we best get going now," says Smee.

Hook finds himself face-to-face with the Tick Tock Croc!

"Smee, what are you waiting for? Row!" yells Hook, dropping the spyglass.

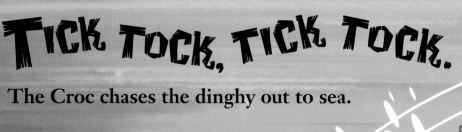

TICK TOCK, TICK TOCK.

The Croc chases the dinghy out to sea.

Why did the pirate give away all his treasure?

"**WHOA!**" says Izzy. "It looks like Hook might never see his spyglass again!"

"That's too bad," says Jake. "If Hook had just asked us if he could borrow our spyglass, we could've helped him."

"It's like you always say, Jake," says Cubby. "You should ask permission before you borrow something that isn't yours."

"I hope that sneaky snook learns his lesson," says Skully.

"Let's head back to Pirate Island," says Jake.

"For solving pirate problems today, we earned gold doubloons," says Jake.

"What are we waiting for?" asks Izzy. "Let's open up the team treasure chest and count them!"

He just had to get it off his chest!

"Cool," says Cubby.

"We earned nine gold doubloons," says Jake.

"Yay-hey, well done, crew," says Izzy.

Squawk to ya later, mateys!

How many sea horses are swimming with Captain Hook?

Help Jake put the gold doubloons in the team treasure chest!

Can you find seven fish in the picture?

Help Captain Hook find his way to safety.

Find eight items that begin with the letter _s_.

Help Cubby find six gold doubloons.

Find five differences between the two scenes.